Entwined in Time

Book One

Taylor Claremont

Gubbins Press

A Note From the Author

Aindreas and Mackenzie's story, while set in Scotland, finds them in a pocket of time in the past. While a hearty attempt was made to keep this book historically accurate, I have never stepped foot in 18th century Scotland and could never possibly pick up on all of the nuances of the time.

I have recorded a tale of bravery, vulnerability, and romance that speaks to all time periods and one that I hope finds its way into your heart. If you're able to suspend your disbelief and not looking for a book that sticks to the history books at a minutely detailed level, come along for the journey and get Entwined in Time with me!

Chapter One

My knees wobbled as I made my way down the hallway that I had walked through daily for the past four years. My boss had summoned me to his office and his voice had held a hint of a smile when he called.

This was it.

I was finally getting promoted.

One of the office's interns stepped out into the hallway as I walked past, and he joined me stride for stride.

"Hey, Kenz."

I cringed at his usage of my nickname. He had been at the company for maybe six months and there was no way we were at nickname status. I smiled tightly and nodded, unable to speak as my nerves churned in my stomach the closer I got to my boss' office.

Oblivious to my nerves, he tried to engage me in conversation. "Bob loved the idea about compiling reports on Thursdays to give us more time to find any errors."

I stopped walking and scowled. That had been my idea for the last two years and every time I brought it up, Bob dismissed it, saying his favorite phrase each time - "Things are done the way they are, and we do things the way they're done."

It was obnoxious and didn't actually make sense. Especially when he claimed to want to grow the business. The intern, Lawrence, had brought me tea a few mornings to chat with me about how the company was run. He had caught me a few times after I left Bob's office fuming, and I shared my ideas with him about what I would do differently. That had been a mistake.

"Coming?"

Lawrence was a few steps ahead of me. Apparently, he had kept talking and only realized I wasn't next to him once I didn't respond. When I caught up to him, he continued on with the story I had missed the beginning of.

"As I was saying, I think I'll be able to make a substantial difference here."

I nodded absentmindedly and gave him a strange look when he walked through Bob's door as I opened it.

"Bob called me in to meet with him. You'll have to wait a minute."

"He called you in to meet with *us*." He emphasized the last word of his sentence and the churning in my stomach threatened to come out.

Before I could question what he meant, Bob walked over to us and clapped Lawrence on the back. The two of them laughed like old chums and I felt awkwardly out of the loop.

"Mackenzie," Bob said, as if he had just noticed me, "say hello to your new supervisor. I'll still be the big boss, of course, but now you'll answer directly to Lawrence."

I forced a smile and reached out behind me to find a chair before my knees gave out. I tried to soothe my nerves, but my mind swirled around as I thought back to the last four years. This was the third time I was passed over for a promotion and I felt sick.

"Now you can share all your *ideas* with him and not waste my time," Bob laughed, and Lawrence joined in.

I sat there, unable to speak and not really believing this was happening. I stared back and forth at the two men and watched in absolute wonder as they congratulated themselves on a job well done.

I had wasted four years of my life and had nothing to show for it. I squeaked out as sincere of a congratulations as I could muster and slipped out of the room. Their banter and laughter carried out into the hallway, and I was certain they hadn't noticed I was gone.

I pressed my hand to the wall to steady myself

and took a deep breath. The long hallway back to my desk looked daunting. I heard an office door open right behind me and I steeled myself, forcing a pained smile across my face.

A warm hand touched my arm and I turned around to see Martha, the building's cleaner. The corners of her eyes were crinkled in a genuine smile, and she patted my arm, "Go to the supply closet and take a moment for yourself."

I hugged her and bit back a sob as I followed her directions. The supply closet was well stocked with enough paper towels and coffee filters to muffle sounds to the outside and I let the tears flow down my face as I got angry about the injustice of Lawrence as my boss.

Pulling out my phone, I hovered over my call list before settling on my boyfriend's number. He would be in the middle of working, but surely he'd be fine taking my call, I convinced myself.

He picked up on the first ring and I let out a sigh of relief.

"Brad, I need to talk. Do you have a minute?"

"Wait, Kenz, I have something I've been wanting to say."

My heart started racing. He had been acting suspicious lately after we stayed up late one night discussing marriage, and he kept saying he was saving his money for something. A ring, obviously. I wiped away my tears and felt hope rising up in me.

Even though I had been passed over for the promotion, maybe this day would turn around after all. But wait, people didn't propose over the phone. I shook my head and realized he was still talking.

"Did you hear me, Mackenzie?"

I bristled at him using my full name, feeling like he was chastising me for not listening.

"It's been a tough morning. What did you say?"

"I said it's over." His voice was devoid of any warmth and carried an edge of annoyance.

People didn't usually propose over the phone, but they also weren't supposed to break up over the phone. I must not have heard him right. We were about to celebrate our third anniversary.

"I found someone new. I guess that doesn't really matter, but I don't know." He was rambling and I collapsed against a stack of paper towels.

"Okay," I said in a small voice and clicked my phone off unceremoniously.

With a numb feeling, I restacked the paper towels and smiled at Martha as she walked in the room.

"Everything okay, dearie? I heard a loud sound."

"I bumped into the stack of paper towels. All better now." I placed the last one on the stack and gave her a quick hug, thanking her for letting me use the closet.

"Can I ask you where you're from?" I asked, hoping my sincere tone wasn't too imposing.

Martha's eyes lit up, and she clasped her hands together. "Scotland."

"Scotland, hm." I smiled at her again and walked to my desk, my mind scrolling through images I had of Scotland. Rolling green hills, cloudy skies, men in kilts.

I grabbed my purse and walked out of the office, not stopping to talk to anyone else on my way to the street.

Hopping into the privacy of my car, I dialed my best friend, Gabby.

"Hey! Happy birthday!!" she screamed into the phone, and I pulled it away from my ear with a wince.

"Oh my gosh, with the day I've had, would you believe I forgot it was my birthday?"

"No! Do we need to meet up?"

"Yes, meet me at my apartment ASAP and bring snacks."

"What's a 'Laird'?" She asked, still eying me suspiciously.

"It was the name given to guys who owned massive amounts of land in Scotland. That's not the important part though," I said, swatting at the air.

"What is the important part?"

"I'm booking a trip for myself!" I looked at her, waiting for her to jump up and start celebrating with me.

"Kenz, have you lost it? I want to be gentle in how I word this- I understand you've had more than a rough day. It's enough to make anyone go crazy, but I don't know what to do if you actually snap."

I laughed and then quieted myself when I heard a little bit of a manic tone at the end of it.

"No, I haven't lost it. If anything, I'm seeing clearly now. I always do what I think is safe. I date the safest guys, I get the safest jobs, I take the least risky route in everything I do. I'm tired of it. This castle looks amazing. Castle Balfour." I let the syllables roll off my tongue and felt a small shiver go through my body that strengthened my resolve.

Gabby worked on a spoonful of ice cream and nodded thoughtfully. I watched her, waiting for a response, and had to practically sit on my hands to keep myself still.

After polishing off another three spoonsful, Gabby nodded again, "I'm coming too."

Her tone was steady and resolute, but her words made excitement bubble up inside of me, and I jumped to my feet. I rushed over and gave her a huge hug while she stared at me.

"Yep, you've lost it. Where's my friend Mackenzie and what have you done with her?"

"This is a new and improved Mackenzie. I will not hold myself back anymore."

To prove I was serious, I pulled up the flight schedule and turned to her, "What's the earliest you can leave?"

She looked startled and pulled out her phone. "I have a meeting I can't miss tomorrow, but after that, I can do whatever I need to do remotely. When do you want to leave?"

"Tomorrow night?"

"Mackenzie!"

I shrugged. "Okay, how about three days from now? We both have passports already and that gives us enough time to pack and whatever."

Her eyes were still wide, but she nodded and started frantically sending emails from her phone.

Chapter Three

I clutched my suitcase as I waited for Gabby to pull up. I had lost some of the steam I had the day I booked our trip, but in my break-up-induced hysteria, I had failed to notice there was no refund policy. Now we were thousands of dollars into this and there was no backing out.

Gabby's car turned the corner at a speed that made me nervous about getting into the car with her. She hopped out and drug my suitcase to her trunk. Her hair was up in a messy bun, and she was clearly dressed to travel comfortably. I was so nervous I hadn't thought of how long the flight would be and looked down at my jeans and button-up shirt.

"Do you think I can change in the airport bathroom?" I mused aloud.

Gabby tugged my hand and guided me into the passenger seat, a grin stretching across her face. "We're about to go to *Scotland* and you're wasting time worrying about changing your clothes? Let's go!"

Somehow, the last three days had the exact opposite effect on my best friend that they had on me. While I was dreading and regretting the decision to go on this trip, she was building up anticipation and excitement that could rival a five-year-old going to Disneyland.

She had blown up my phone with message after message about local customs and places we needed to go check out. Once she exhausted all the places within a day's drive of Castle Balfour, she began sending me pictures of guys in kilts.

Now she was racing us toward the airport, and I was sitting in the passenger seat, biting my nails and worried about all the rash decisions I had made the last few days. Right after I booked the trip, I called up Bob and quit. No notice, no beating around the bush. I called and spat out my resignation with a determination and resolve that scared me a little bit. It scared Bob a little bit, too. He ended the call with a "yes ma'am" that, not going to lie, made me feel more alive than ever.

Now that the adrenaline rush of that had worn off, I was formulating an apology email and trying to figure out which words sounded more sincere. I didn't necessarily want my job back, but I didn't want to come home from Scotland broke and single.

Gabby was quite convinced I'd meet a modern-day Laird who would sweep me off my feet and we'd live in his castle filled with piles and piles of gold. A cartoon version of her fantasy ran through my head, and I wanted to laugh it off, but what a relief would that be? I would have never guessed I would be single, jobless, and on my way to Scotland just days after turning twenty-five.

I groaned and grabbed the dashboard as Gabby came to a screeching halt.

She flashed me an apologetic look, "Sorry, the other drivers don't seem to get that we're on our way to Scotland."

"It's not your driving, although I wouldn't be sad if you slowed down a little bit."

She gave me a sheepish grin and picked her speed back up as the traffic in front of us dispersed.

"What's on your mind?"

"This was a huge mistake."

"Kenz, making mistakes is a big part of life. But this wasn't a mistake, I promise you."

"What if it was, though?"

"Then learn from it. We're only a few minutes from the airport." She was practically squealing with delight and looked at me expectantly.

Wanting her to get her eyes back on the road, I gave her a shaky smile and braced myself for our arrival.

I said a silent prayer of gratitude as Gabby slowed down through the winding airport roads. Although I was certain it was simply a calculated maneuver as she weighed the option of speeding through and getting a ticket or kicked out versus following the posted speed and getting to our flight without hassle.

"Kenz!" Her shout startled me, and I hit my head on the door frame as I stepped out of the car.

"What? What is it?" I turned around in alarm, expecting to see the car on fire.

"We're at the *airport*."

This was going to be a long trip.

Chapter Four

"That's Ben Macdui up ahead. I hiked it nae two months ago. Do you hike?"

The driver Castle Balfour sent was trying to engage me in conversation, but I couldn't peel my eyes away from the landscape. All fears that this was a mistake went out the window when I stepped outside and saw the rugged landscape around me. The air was fresh and crisp, like the first delicious days of autumn. The sun was just peeking out behind thick clouds that were rapidly dispersing, giving way to the purest blue sky I had ever seen.

Our driver, a young man named John, informed us we had just missed a torrential downpour and were blessed to be seeing the highlands in all its glory. Gabby was smitten with his accent, and I kept deferring to her any time he asked a question. Finally, he took the hint and turned all his attention on her.

Left to myself, I stared out at the jagged rocks poking out of the emerald grass in ways that had to have been placed by ancient gods at the beginning of time. There was a mystical feeling to the air that made me shiver, despite the heat blasting from the car's vents. It felt like coming home and like adventure all at the same time. Maybe this was what taking risks and getting out of my comfort zone felt like.

"Nae, many people come to Castle Balfour on such short notice. What brings you here?"

"We saw pictures and fell in love. And maybe we'll fall in love in other ways too," Gabby shamelessly winked at the driver who blushed the deepest shade of red I've yet to see in my life.

I snorted and suddenly the attention was back on me.

"You don't believe in love?"

I squirmed in my seat. "I didn't say that. I just guess I haven't found it yet, and I thought I had."

"Aye, that would make a person doubt." He looked at me in the review mirror with sympathy and I looked down at my hands, not wanting to betray the tears in my eyes.

He and Gabby chatted, and I let the sounds of their voices fade to background noise, getting lost in the views as we wound through the countryside. Every turn took my breath away, and I wanted to keep asking if this was a dream, but I kept it to myself.

"'ere we are," John said, and I squinted in confusion when I looked forward and only saw a thick patch of trees ahead of us. Before I could ask what he meant, he laughed, "Well, we're almost there. I get excited when I see the trees. Used to play in them when I was but a wee bairn."

"Are you part of the Balfour family?" I asked.

"Nae, I have always wished, but alas, my father's line is Clan Campbell. A strong ally of the Balfours, but not blood kin. You'll meet my mam when you get settled in. She's a Brit and comes across mighty harsh, but a lovely woman once you get to know her," He winked at Gabby, who fluttered her eyelashes and blushed.

In a dense forest silence, we wound through the trees, each one looking ancient and weather-worn while standing tall and proud, like soldiers protecting the castle from being seen from the road. When one final turn brought us to the gates, I couldn't imagine the castle being any finer than the ornate stonework framing the gate. As the time-tested hinges creaked open, the car crawled through, and it felt like I was transported to another time.

For being over five hundred years old, the castle looked immaculate and welcoming. It wasn't stiff and cold like I imagined it would be. Smoke swirled out of several chimneys and most of the windows were decorated with a candle or two, making it feel like we were being welcomed home after a long journey.

Gabby gasped and turned around to grab my arm.

"Kenz! We're here!"

I smiled and nodded, unable to take my eyes away from the castle towering above us. John helped both of us out of the car and directed a bellhop to grab our bags.

"You'll go right through those doors and mam will find you. Oy, there she is now." He waved enthusiastically at a woman wearing a tight bun and a formal gown. She waved back courteously enough, but I felt a little apprehensive about being in her care for the next two weeks.

"The others are already in the study," she said, hastily ushering us in the door.

I paid too much money for this trip to be rushed through it, so I hung back and took my time following her to the rest of the group. The castle had an earthy smell that was familiar in a way I couldn't place. I took in a deep inhale and realized it reminded me of playing in my grandma's garden when I was little. A mix of stone and dirt that felt like childhood.

We walked past room after room and my eyes couldn't take all of it in fast enough. I made note of a long hallway that looked like it was filled with paintings and artifacts that I wanted to spend more time in later. It wasn't exactly men in kilts so I would have to come up with some strong persuasion to convince Gabby to join me.

Entering the study, I saw three other people, individuals who had come on this journey alone. They sat apart from each other, taking up most of the sitting area, forcing Gabby and I to sit on opposite ends of the room or stand up if we wanted to be by each other. We huddled in the back corner and stood nervously after attempting to smile at the other guests and receiving blank stares back.

Mrs. Campbell quickly passed out thick packets to each of us. *Margaret* was written at the top of mine and I stepped forward to hand it back to her.

"There's been a mistake, my name isn't Margaret, it's Mackenzie."

She threw the back of her hand across her forehead and sighed, "Not here it isn't. The Clan Mackenzie was one of the biggest enemies of Clan Balfour. Here you will be known as Margaret."

"What about Clan Campbell?" I retorted under my breath.

There was fire behind Mrs. Campbell's eyes that made me avert my own as she answered a question I hadn't meant for her to hear. "The Campbells came to the rescue of Clan Balfour in the 18th century. We have remained allies ever since. That is why the current Laird of this castle trusts me to oversee these experiences, even if I am only English."

I nodded and wished I could shrink myself into the whisky bottle sitting on the table. Her harsh stare bore through the top of my head, and I physically felt relief when she looked away. I let out my breath and Gabby squeezed my arm, raising her eyebrows in sympathy.

"Will we get to meet the current Laird?" Gabby asked and received a worse look than I did.

"If he graces us with his presence, perhaps. I am not his keeper."

It was my turn to squeeze Gabby's arm in solidarity. Nowhere on the website did it say the host was a sour woman who made the castle feel like a punishment. My feelings of regret started bubbling back up and I had a tough time concentrating on Mrs. Campbell's words.

I caught the end of a sentence as she dismissed everyone to their rooms and hoped the packets contained a map. Flipping through the pages quickly, I was relieved to find a hand drawn and well-marked layout of the entire castle grounds.

"Shall we go, Margaret?"

"Did you get to keep your name? Gabby isn't exactly Scottish."

Gabby shrugged and showed me her name scrawled across the top. It figured. I started to walk to the room number that was written on my paper and noticed it was in an entirely different wing than Gabby's.

"So much for a vacation together," I murmured.

Chapter Five

I woke up to birds singing and sat upright, unsure of where I was. In the city, a car horn was far more likely to wake me up than any wildlife. Rubbing my eyes, I looked around at the stone walls and fell back on the bed as I remembered I was in Scotland.

My phone buzzed on the antique nightstand next to me.

Meet me downstairs in like 30? Foyer?

I peeled myself out of the warm bed and shivered as my feet hit the cold area rug. The stone floor I touched with my next step was even worse. I should have brought slippers. Maybe there would be a store in town that had some.

I tried to get hot water out of the old plumbing in the shower and settled on splashing my face with icy water and cleaning the rest of my body as quickly as humanly possible. The towels were a welcome softness and plushness in stark contrast to the rough bathing experience.

Running a comb through my hair, I put on the smallest amount of makeup to help my face seem a little more alive and less a victim of jetlag than it currently looked in the cloudy mirror above the sink.

Satisfied with my appearance, I threw on a black turtleneck sweater and fleece-lined leggings and slipped my feet into tennis shoes. Mrs. Campbell would probably have something to say to me about my outfit, but I had a feeling she'd find something wrong even if I had shown up in authentic period pieces.

I made my way down the hallway and stopped abruptly when I couldn't remember if I was supposed to go left or right. I ran back to my room and grabbed the map off the nightstand. Looking down at it to determine my path, I bumped into another guest coming out of his room. He was dressed in a kilt and looked so at home, I thought he was an actor for the castle.

"Sorry," I mumbled and tried to walk past him without giving him an opportunity to chat.

He started to say something, but the look on my face must've made him think twice. He closed his mouth and nodded briefly to me. When I nodded back, I noticed he looked like he had seen a ghost. As much as I didn't want to stop and talk, I was now curious about what had actually stopped him from talking. I wasn't given the chance to ask him as he bustled down the hallway in front of me and never slowed down or turned around.

Shaking my head, I returned to my study of the map. I was thankful for a semi-photographic memory, so I wouldn't have to carry it around with me all the time. I wasn't like some of those geniuses that can glance at a paper and recite every letter and comma on it, but I could study something with intense focus for a few moments and easily recall it later.

My attention kept returning to a hall marked Balfour Ulaidh. My curiosity got the best of me, and I pulled out my phone to translate what it meant. *Treasure.* I ran through a tour of the castle in my mind and figured out it was the hallway I had made a note of when we first came in. I could easily go through the hall and meet Gabby before she started looking for me.

I had barely made my way into the hall when a painting at the end of the display caught my eye. The man in it looked to be in his mid-twenties, close to my age, his face worn, but proud looking. His blue eyes tugged at my heart in a way no painting ever had before.

I read the plaque beneath his portrait and sighed -

Aindreas Balfour c. 1722

Laird of Balfour Castle. Repeatedly survived attacks to protect his family, his castle, and his lands. A brave, beloved warrior of the people.

Just that little bit of information made me wonder more about the sadness behind his eyes. For a twenty-three-year-old, his face carried a worry and heaviness that made something inside me ache.

"Kenz! Check this out!" Gabby had found me and pulled me away. I turned around to look into Aindreas Balfour's alluring blue eyes once more before I was whisked around the corner.

My breath caught in my throat at what she wanted to show me. It was another painting of Aindreas Balfour. He was a child in this one, standing with a calf laying at his feet, looking up at him with adoration in its eyes. My heart melted more than a little, and I wished I could reach out and give the little boy a hug to shield him from his tumultuous future. In this painting, his eyes carried none of the heaviness that the previous one showed.

"Oh man, we need to go. Look how close it is to ten." Gabby pointed up to an antique clock groaning as it kept up with the time resentfully, sounding like each tick would be its last.

"Is that what time the dress fitting is?"

"Honestly, Kenz! Have you paid attention at all?"

I shook my head, "I've been trying, but I'm not doing a great job of 'fully immersing' myself."

"Well, talk to me, my friend," Gabby laced her arm through mine and we made our way to the fitting.

"I've still been regretting the trip a little bit. I don't regret it now that we're here and it's so beautiful, but I'm scared. I've never been in this position before and I don't know how things will turn out. So, I guess I'm not really jumping in. It seems like too big of a commitment."

She gave my arm a light squeeze and leaned in, "We'll be here for the next two weeks so why not dive in with me and see how much fun we can have? When have we ever been able to just enjoy ourselves without any responsibilities?"

She had a point. I couldn't remember the last time I was able to fully let go and not worry about the next day. I squeezed her arm back and nodded as we entered a large room that had been converted into a sewing room.

Measuring tapes, thread, fabric, and pins were strewn about the room and a harried looking man with a pencil tucked behind his ear ran back and forth, clucking and hemming and hawing over the work of three young women who were frantically measuring and cutting fabric still attached to the guests. They were ensuring the absolute best fit possible and it was awe-inspiring to see the detail and care that went into each outfit.

When it was my turn to be poked and measured, and jostled around by the seamstress in charge of my dress, I looked over at Gabby and we started giggling and couldn't stop. This earned us a sharp over-the-glasses look from the man running about. His intense attitude only added to our giggles, and we tried desperately, but in vain, to cover up our unappreciated joy.

The abrupt clearing of a throat made us stand at attention, making it substantially easier for the women to put our outfits together. Mrs. Campbell had walked in without us seeing and clearly did not like that we kept laughing. I coughed from holding in the giggles that wanted to spill out. She was a ridiculously foreboding character, and I could hardly believe our driver, John, was genuinely her son.

She cleared her throat again and all eyes were instantly on her.

"Today's agenda includes visiting the village square. It's much the same as it would have been five hundred or more years ago. We've kept it intact and there are a few shops that have been passed down through generations of the same family. One such shop is the jewelry store. While it wasn't exactly a Zales in the 17th century, it was a blacksmith and was owned by a lengthy line of blacksmiths-turned-jewelers. They're the McMillans. The produce stand has many heirloom strains of vegetables that have been preserved throughout the years as well. We leave in thirty minutes, sharp."

Gabby leaned over and whispered in my ear, "I thought this would be a little more laid back. Who knew the Scots were so uptight?"

Mrs. Campbell shot us a harsh look and I put my hand on my corset to steady my breathing before I broke out into laughter.

Her voice turned serious and foreboding. "If you are talked to, it is wise to be constantly aware of the fact you are a guest of the Balfour family. Behave as such and hold people to the same standard as they talk to you."

I nodded solemnly and noticed she was looking me directly in the eye. I averted my eyes, taken aback by the intensity, and swallowed hard as all the threat of giggles passed quickly from my system.

Chapter Six

Our heavy skirts swished around our ankles and our satchels clinked with coins as we trekked to the village square. I stared around in wonder at what I assumed were perfectly authentic vendors. Every person there was dressed and talking as though they were preserved in a little pocket of space untouched by time. I could smell food cooking up ahead and I let my nose lead the way.

The hired actors moved about the cobblestone streets nimbly like it was no harder than walking in a flat field. I, on the other hand, felt each bump in the road and tripped on at least every third step. A villager walked past and turned to his companion as he scoffed in my direction, "That lass be mad wae it."

The absurdity of it made me giggle and stumble on another cobblestone. Gabby swiftly grabbed my arm, "*Have* you been drinking?"

"No! I can't manage these blasted stones in these shoes. How do you do it?"

"I walk as if each step is across a vast ocean of clouds."

She clasped her hand to her heart and sighed as I rolled my eyes and tripped over another stone.

"Where should we go first?" Gabby's eyes were lit up at the sight of all the vendors and shops. I quickly deferred to her for direction, even as my stomach grumbled.

"Wherever you want to go first, I'm good with, just walk slower! And make sure we make it to food soon."

"Oh! There's the jewelry store that used to be a blacksmith. Let's start there."

I nodded and looked down at my feet in vain. I couldn't see them through my skirt and had no idea how I'd get to the store in one piece. Gabby grabbed my arm and steered me through the people and down the street, as sure as if her feet had walked this path a thousand times.

A small bell chimed to alert the jeweler of our arrival. An old woman with kind eyes and a warm smile bustled out from a back room. The scent that filled the shop was something that could only come from a building centuries old. There were glass jewelry cases near the register that seemed so out of place in such an old shop. I glanced over their contents briefly, mostly pieces that were clearly stocked to appeal to tourists, but none caught my attention.

Gabby chatted with the woman as I walked father back into an area with sunlight filtering in through an old window. I put my hand out and let the light play across my skin. In this corner, without modern lights or display cases to distract, it looked as if time stood still. I watched the stream of sunlight with wonder and noticed it looked like a spotlight.

Following where it landed, I saw a golden necklace on a rough card of paper. It had no markings on the tag to indicate its price or significance, which seemed odd given the thoroughly cataloged information of every other piece I saw on my way in.

I reached out and then pulled my hand back when a voice behind me startled me.

"Aye, tis a braw piece of jewelry. Tis a shame, in all my years not one person has come in and laid their hands upon it. My mam used to tell me tales about it. She would say, Isla-" Her eyes grew wide as if she had suddenly remembered a terrifying memory, and I put my hands down to smooth my skirt.

"Nae, pick it up. You are the one Lady Balfour foretold." Her voice came out in a shaky whisper that unsettled me to my core and made me freeze.

The woman's face was pale, and her hands trembled as she pressed the necklace into my hand. I felt a surge of nerves course through my body as the pendant made contact with my palm. I convinced myself it was simply that the old woman had thrown me off guard and reached into my satchel to pay for it. She quickly threw up her hand and stopped me.

Her voice was barely above a whisper, and I had to strain forward to hear all of what she said.

"Tis already yours, no need to pay for it. Put the necklace on before you sleep and wish for the one that has your heart. You will find him before you wake."

I thanked her and noticed the color only returned to her face when I promised to follow her instruction exactly.

Back out on the street, I turned to Gabby and shook my head. "I know this is an immersive experience, but dang, that woman really made me think Lady Balfour told her I'd be coming."

"That was insane. I can't wait to see what the rest of the experience is like!"

We linked arms and made our way around to each merchant, stopping to smell fragrant flowers a group of children were selling. Gabby bought a few and tucked them into our hair.

"No clue if that's authentic," she said with a shrug, sniffing the single flower that remained in her hand.

I shrugged and slipped across the stones to a merchant selling tartans. I ran my fingers across the textures and marveled at the designs.

"What one would you like, mistress?"

"Oh, I'm just looking."

"It looks like you've got a beautiful earasaid on already." He tipped his head to me and turned to the next customer.

I looked down at my skirts and had to admit the pattern was pretty. It was deep blue with orange, yellow, and light blue woven through it. I had seen the same pattern all over the castle and assumed it was the tartan pattern for the Balfour family.

Now that I had been in Scotland for more than a day, I started to feel the reverence and pull of this place. The air felt pregnant with magic, and history didn't repeat itself – it was still being lived out. The best parts of it anyway. I didn't see any battles or bloodshed on our way to the market.

There was still an intense pride for the Balfour family in this area and I was certain they had been an integral part in helping this area survive and thrive after the uprisings I had read about. Other Clans didn't survive in the same numbers that Clan Balfour achieved.

Gabby pulled me out of my contemplation and down the street to where we could smell food. We both ordered large steaming bowls of pottage with bannocks and smeared them with golden yellow butter. Our meal came with a jug of whisky that we planned on drinking like pirates. With a lot of sweating and coordinated effort, we got control of our outfits enough to sit at a picnic table.

"Now that I'm hot, I'm not sure if I want soup," Gabby groaned.

I was hungry enough that I didn't care about the temperature of my food or myself. I broke off some of the biscuit and scooped it into the soup. The ingredients looked simple, but the flavors came together in a hearty, grounding way that I couldn't get enough of. Polishing off my first bowl, I made my way back over to the food stall to order another bowl.

The man behind the counter grinned at me, recognizing me easily from having been there five minutes prior, "Aye, my mam was known for this recipe. She said it was passed down through generations and used to be served in the castle on the regular."

"Well, it's delicious. My compliments to the chef," I grinned, and he blushed as he busied himself with getting my bowl refilled, along with another jug of whisky.

Without spilling a drop, I made my way back over to Gabby and inhaled the aroma of the pottage as if it were my first bowl. She was just finishing up her food as I took my last bite of my second helping.

"Ready for more shops?"

I put my hand on my belly and groaned, "Can't we wait a minute?"

She harumphed and folded her arms.

"Okay, fine," I forced myself to a standing position and was convinced I'd wear out the leather of my shoes as we walked around to every stall and every shop.

With aching feet and arms filled with treasure, we made our way back to the castle as the sun set around us. The walk felt surreal. I wasn't convinced we hadn't time traveled somehow or, if not that, that we'd found ourselves on the set of a movie.

My shopping bag bought to contain all my purchases was the only thing that looked out of place and brought me back to reality as I collapsed onto my bed, too tired to remove even my shoes.

A second later, the jeweler's face flashed across my mind and my eyes snapped open. I grabbed the necklace out of my bag and put it on. I didn't have the energy to get up and check myself out in the mirror. I'd have to do that the next morning. I pressed my hand to the pendant, pressing it into the flesh of my chest, and closed my eyes.

"Take me to my true love."

I kept one eye firmly shut while I peeked open my other eye. As I expected, no man was standing in my room, and it looked the exact same as it had when I closed my eyes.

I blew out the candle on my nightstand and fell asleep easily, my hand resting against the pendant.

Chapter Seven

I woke up to birds outside my window again. This time, I knew exactly where I was. I laid in bed for a moment, refusing to open my eyes, still aching from the hours of walking we had done around the village.

I had dreamt about a faceless man all night and didn't want reality to hit me just yet, but my body had other ideas. Unable to ignore my bladder any longer, I begrudgingly opened my eyes to a disorienting darkness. The dreams were so real, I half expected to feel a man lying in bed next to me, but there was no one.

I smoothed down the blanket as I stepped out of bed and my eyes refused to adjust to the darkness of the room. The morning felt even more chilly than the one prior and I pulled my shawl more tightly around me. I forgot to get slippers the day before, but at least my shoes were still on, and the coldness of the floor didn't shock me as badly as it had the morning before. I couldn't fathom how cold I would have been if I would have taken the time to undress the night before. I shivered at the thought of being in a thin nightgown and straightened my dress up in the dark.

Stretching my hands out, I felt for the nightstand so I could grab my phone and use its flashlight to guide me. I didn't feel anything, so I reached out farther. Still nothing. I sat back on the bed and centered myself. My sleepy eyes were starting to adjust to the room, but nothing seemed right. The fireplace in the corner wasn't there. The doorway to the bathroom looked wrong.

There were thick drapes on the window that I didn't remember being there. Pulling a corner up, daylight flooded in the room, and I gasped when I realized I was on the ground level. I had somehow sleepwalked or something and, based on the contents of the room, someone was currently staying in it.

I heard a noise outside the door and quickly dropped the corner of the curtain. The room was enshrouded in darkness again and I frantically felt around for a lamp or a way out. I shuffled towards the sound of the door and was about to reach out for a handle when the door flew open. A large figure ran in and quickly shut the door before I could see who it was.

"Who's there?" a deep voice with a thick Scottish accent called out in a forced whisper.

I stumbled forward and yelped as my toe hit the corner of the bed. A small burst of firelight quickly broke up the darkness as the man attached to the voice lit a candle.

It illuminated the room just enough to see a rough outline of the man in front of me. He picked up the candle from a handmade table and the flickers of light cast shadows along his face as he studied me.

"Hi, I'm Mackenzie," I extended my hand out and he backed up into the wall as if I had just pulled a gun out of my pocket.

"You're a what?"

I must have made it down to the actors' wing. This guy was really in character. I thought back to Mrs. Campbell's harshness when I said my name was Mackenzie and I quickly corrected myself.

"Oh, I mean, I'm Margaret?"

He looked at me suspiciously, "Are you a Mackenzie? Answer me truthful. I dinnae want to hurt a lass, so you're safe. But if you're here to trick me, it won't work."

I shook my head and put my palms out to show I had nothing to hide. Stepping slowly and deliberately towards him, I lowered my voice and played along, "My last name is Clark. I don't know anyone from Clan Mackenzie."

He furrowed his brows. The thickness of them accentuated by the shadows from the candle and stared at my hands before looking me up and down.

My cheeks flushed at such intense attention. I was thankful the light was dim enough he wouldn't be able to see the change in color.

"Where are you from?"

"The States."

His brows furrowed more deeply than I could have imagined a person's brows could furrow.

"Manhattan," I added, hoping that would clear up the confusion. His brows became one entity with that answer.

"New York?" Now I was questioning my own sanity. Was I from New York? My head started pounding, and I desperately looked around for any sign of a water tap. I shouldn't have drunk more whisky than water in the village, but when everyone was calling it *uisge beatha*, the water of life, and handing me glass after glass as we walked around when the day got hotter, it was hard to refuse.

"I dinnae wish to be rude, but I don't understand where you're from. Your accent is brisk and impossible." He shrugged and I sighed in frustration.

He thought I was hard to understand? His accent was thick and laced with enough Gaelic words that I was having a challenging time picking out words I recognized.

A loud sound erupted outside, and he blew the candle out.

He dropped his voice, "We'll figure it out later,

41

TAYLOR CLAREMONT

come with me."

He grasped my hand and pulled me out of the door into a small alleyway. I blamed my hangover for the butterflies in my stomach.

Turning around, I saw I had woken up in a cottage, not the castle. Had I gone home with a Scottish guy the night before and couldn't remember? He didn't seem like he was unsafe, and the mysterious edge was a little hot, but I had woken up enough to know I was in a sketchy situation. I checked my skirts for any sign of my phone to no avail. It was nowhere to be found, and I was certain the cottage we just left didn't have electricity, much less a landline.

"We should be safe out here, but keep your voice low."

I blinked a few times as my eyes adjusted to the light outside. The smells were different than the day before, more authentic. I smelled hay and saw enormous quantities of it being carted by at the end of the alleyway.

"Where are we?" I looked around in amazement. This village was slightly different than the one we visited the day before and its citizens were far more committed to the illusion.

He didn't turn around, but whispered just loud enough for me to hear, "How do you dinnae ken where you are? And keep yourself quieter."

I fell in line behind him, even though a million

questions were running through my mind. Something about the seriousness in his voice made me listen to him. He had a commanding air that probably helped him get his way a lot.

As we cautiously walked between buildings, my thoughts drifted to Lawrence and how he could learn a thing or two from this guy. And then I was seething. I had been distracted enough the last two days to forget about everything in the hustle and bustle of traveling. Now that I was left alone with my thoughts and couldn't talk, I thought about how things were going at work and how Lawrence was sitting in an office that should have been mine.

"Your face is red, drink."

The man had turned around and was shoving a flask in my direction. I looked up and all the blood rushed out of my body. It was effective for relieving my headache, but did nothing to help me otherwise.

He looked at me quizzically, and I pushed my thoughts aside. There was no way it was possible.

"Aindreas?" I whispered.

He stopped dead in his tracks. "Ye ken my name. How?"

"I read it. I mean, I don't know. I need a minute." My headache was back as I tried to figure out how Aindreas Balfour was standing in front of me. I took a swig from the flask and cleared my throat.

"A minute is something we don't have." He

reached out to get the flask back and I stood frozen in place. A painting had come to life in front of me and I couldn't force myself to move.

"Are the men after us real?"

"Of course they're real."

"Why are they after us?"

He let out an exasperated sigh as he realized I wasn't going anywhere until I had some answers.

"They're nae after you. They recognized me."

"But why does that matter? Shouldn't they be bowing to you or something?"

He scoffed and a rough laugh came out, "That would be the day."

"You own these lands, though. You're the Laird."

A pained look darkened his face. "Aye, but I haven't been for long. And there are people who would rather me dead than their Laird."

"Why?" I whispered.

"I'd really rather we discussed this while we kept our feet moving."

He turned around to walk again, and I picked up my pace to follow him.

Chapter Eight

"So they say you killed your father and they're after you to avenge his death?"

We had stopped for the night and Aindreas built a fire after he surveyed the area thoroughly and determined there was no threat.

"Aye," he stared at the flames and the light danced in his eyes, softening them, although his face was held in a hard grimace.

"And you didn't?"

He turned toward me, the fire still in his eyes, "Nae, but I held his dying body in my arms." He gazed down at his arms, no doubt seeing his father's last moments.

"I'm so sorry," I whispered, and reached out to touch his arm. The touch startled him a little, and I pulled my hand back.

"Do you still have your parents?"

"Yes, but we don't have a good relationship."

"Aye, so we have something in common. I dinnae like the man. He was cruel and harsh when I was young, but I would nae kill him."

The pain on his face pulled at my heart and I wished I could reach out and hug him, but I sat on my hands instead. The fire was dying out, so Aindreas threw another log on. Within seconds, it was crackling and popping. I pulled my hands back out and rubbed them together to warm them up.

If I ever made it back to the future, I wouldn't complain about the coldness of the castle ever again. At least it was a roof over my head. I looked up, imagining a better canopy protecting me from the elements, and gasped when I saw the sky. With no light pollution around, the stars were thick and visible.

"What is it?" He tilted his head upwards to see what had taken my breath away and didn't see anything.

"I had no idea there were that many stars."

"They dinnae have stars where you come from?" He laughed heartily, and I joined in at the absurdness of it all.

"Not this many."

"I dinnae get where you're from, Margaret. Tis an odd place if it dinnae have as many stars. We should all have the same sky."

I continued looking up at the stars, trying to find the points of various constellations I had only read about. In New York, we didn't exactly have a chance to stargaze like this. And on the odd night star gazing seemed like a better option than television, I would spend forever trying to find The Big Dipper before giving up. Out here, there were stars upon stars.

"We have more light. It drowns them out."

"That sounds awful."

"It really is."

My eyes were growing heavy, being lulled to sleep by the cracking fire and the peacefulness of sitting outside in a still, quiet world. Aindreas helped me get settled on a patch of grass that was cool and hard. He grasped my hand and guided me back as my skirt made the task infinitely more difficult than it would have been in pants. Still, the extra fabric provided warmth that leggings would have never been able to.

"If I fall asleep, dinnae worry. I wake up at the slightest sound. You'll be safe."

I trusted him and let my weary eyes close.

The next thing I knew, Aindreas was standing over me. I stretched and started to say something. He put his hand up and placed his finger over his mouth. He pointed off to the side of where we had been sleeping. Listening closely, I heard horses in the distance.

"We have enough time to stay ahead of them if we go now," he whispered, and we were off.

Aindreas led us through trails and woods like he knew the area with his eyes closed. We covered a lot of ground, but we were at a disadvantage without horses, and I wasn't sure how much longer I'd be able to walk with no end in sight. I was hungry, thirsty, and my feet were blistered.

Aindreas forged ahead as my steps grew weaker and weaker. He turned around and rushed over to me, his eyes worried, reminding me of the portrait in the hall at Castle Balfour.

"Go on without me," I said, waving him away.

"There'll be none of that," he said, scooping me up. I had no strength to fight him. I rested my heavy head against his chest. He smelled like campfire and fresh air and his walking quickly lulled me back to sleep.

I woke up to the sound of three men arguing and I tried to hold as still as possible. I could make out Aindreas' voice, but the other two I hadn't heard before.

"Your lass is awake," one of the unfamiliar voices muttered.

Caught, I opened my eyes and found myself in a decent-sized room. A fire was blazing in the corner and there were plates of food upon a table that the three men were sitting at. Aindreas rushed over and knelt down beside me.

"Sorry about this. We made it to my cousin's

home, and it was the safest place I could think of to get you. Eat up."

He helped me to my feet and walked with me over to the table.

One of the men snorted. "What's wrong with you, cousin. She can help herself." He turned his attention to me, and my skin bristled. "Grab some food and then head in the kitchen with my wife and the other women."

If I hadn't been on the brink of starvation, I would've thrown the food at him and left the house. As it was, I did not know where I was or when I would have food in front of me again, so I did my best to grab a decent-looking biscuit and started eating it in pieces. I turned to Aindreas, pleading with my eyes that he would step in.

Aindreas looked at me and then turned to his cousin, "She stays here with me."

The man threw his hands up, "Aye, you're the Laird."

Something about the way he said Laird made my stomach drop. He had no respect for Aindreas, and it made me furious. Certain that this wasn't the time for a public outcry against this man, I did my best to swallow the dry bites of biscuit that I couldn't seem to soften in my mouth.

He walked out of the room, shouting something in Gaelic to an unseen person down the hall.

"That was my cousin, Magnus. He's been helping me adjust to being Laird and working on getting the local clans back on my side."

I turned my attention to the other person in the room and saw that he was a short, mousy, balding man who had to be at least twenty years older than Aindreas. He had a sour look on his face and cleared his throat.

"Ah, where are my manners? This is Richard. He was my father's most trusted man and now he's mine."

I nodded, unable to speak for fear of spraying crumbs everywhere.

"You can use butter, ye ken?"

Aindreas pointed to the pat of butter a foot from the biscuits, and I sheepishly spread some across my food. It helped the rest of the biscuit go down much more easily.

"So if this man was your father's advisor and now he's yours, that means he trusts you weren't responsible for his death?"

"Oh nae," Richard spoke up, pushing his glasses up the bridge of his nose as he stepped closer to me, lowering his voice, "I was with Aindreas when Laird Balfour, sorry, the former Laird Balfour, was murdered. Ah ken he didn't do it."

Aindreas nodded, "And Magnus is my closest living family. He's been out scouting around the countryside, looking for anyone that has answers."

"Clearing Aindreas' name is our number one priority," Richard wrung his hands and looked at me nervously, "And you're sure we can trust her?"

"Aye, I've never felt like I could trust someone more."

The sincerity in his eyes made me blush, and I looked down at the ground.

Richard shook his head with a sad smile. "That's your greatest asset, Aindreas, and your biggest problem. You're too trusting."

Chapter Nine

By the next morning, I wasn't as surprised to wake up in a new place. It seemed like that was the way things would be for the foreseeable future, or was it the foreseeable past?

It was hard keeping my secret time travel from Aindreas. I had only known him for two days, but he was so open and generous. I felt awful keeping something so huge from him. I had seen enough movies and read enough books to know that I couldn't just blurt it out. I fretted about the room, thinking of ways I could approach the subject, and nothing sounded sane. He was trusting, but he wasn't stupid.

I made my way to the main living area and was surprised to see that Magnus' home had servants milling about. To me, it seemed like a lot of people and when I remarked on it, Richard told me in a hushed voice that Castle Balfour had at least ten times as many. I pictured the layout of the castle and tried to imagine that many people. It had to feel like a constant buzz of activity that never slowed down.

Aindreas, Magnus, and Richard spent several

hours behind closed doors, their voices occasionally rising and falling. I begrudgingly stayed in the kitchen, trying my best to keep to myself and answer any questions as minimally as possible.

The head of the kitchen found it very odd I didn't know my way around.

"A widow like you should 'ave some experience wit a blade," a woman with muscular forearms that would put the most bulked up athletes to shame tisked at me as she walked by carrying a large bowl of dough.

That was the other thing. Everyone who came across me assumed I was a widow of some sort. Aindreas and Richard were the only two who made no remark about my marital status or age.

I stared longingly at the door they were behind, hoping they'd come out before the sun went down.

"Take this in there," one of the women shoved a platter of assorted foods into my arms and steered me towards the door.

I walked in silently, relieved to see Aindreas and hoping my presence wouldn't bring any more unwanted talking from Magnus.

"'ere she is now," Magnus said, standing up and opening his arms in a wide gesture that made me freeze.

Aindreas jumped up and grabbed the platter from me with a nod and a smile that made my stomach flutter. I gave him a quick smile and turned to walk out of the room.

"Wait right there," Magnus' voice boomed, and I turned back around slowly.

"How do we know she's not a spy?"

Aindreas stepped forward, shielding me from Magnus' direct line of sight.

"She's nae a spy."

"Then explain why she's here with you."

Aindreas and I hadn't really had a chance to discuss anything enough for me to come up with a plausible reason I was traveling alone in the 18th century. I fumbled over my words and tried to put together something coherent. As words that made no sense spilled out of my mouth, I grabbed for the necklace, hoping the familiarity of it would bring some comfort.

Aindreas' eyes widened, and he stepped closer to me. He put his hand over mine and whispered in a voice low enough for only me to hear, "Hide the necklace and dinnae let anyone see it."

I tucked it back under the fabric of my dress and walked out of the room before Magnus could grill me any further. Clicking the door shut behind me, I heard their voices raise again.

I pressed my hand to my necklace through the fabric, wondering why it brought out such a reaction in Andreas.

"They dinnae like the food?" the woman who handed me the platter was standing against the wall, her arms folded and a smirk on her face.

"They liked the food just fine," I snapped back.

She unfolded her arms and stepped towards me as if she were going to smack me. I shrunk back and put my hands out. I didn't know how long I would be in this time and I figured I should try to play nice.

"I'm sorry. It's been a long couple of days."

The woman sized me up and down and pursed her lips. "I suppose a lady of pleasure is nae used to so much walking and being upright."

My cheeks burned. I may not have known exactly what everyone was saying all the time, but *lady of pleasure* was more than easy to figure out.

"I'm not-"

"Oh, dinnae waste your breath. None of us care. Ah ken it would only be a matter of time before Aindreas would find one of you."

"*Laird Balfour* has been nothing but hospitable and a gentleman to me," I retorted back, no longer caring if this woman was my friend or not.

"We shall see. How much is he paying you? Magnus says his money is dwindling fast, so enjoy it while you can."

A young man with a letter came running through the house and burst through the doors, keeping the men's conversation private. A few seconds later, Aindreas came out looking panicked.

"Margaret, get your things together. We're leaving right now."

I rushed to the room I had stayed the night in and grabbed my satchel. I looked around and realized I had nothing else to grab. I ran out to the courtyard and found Aindreas and Richard each on their own horses.

"Have you ridden before?"

I shook my head, and he walked his horse over to me. With one quick motion, he grabbed me around the waist and hoisted me up onto the horse's back, cozied right in front of him.

With his hips keeping me firmly on the horse and his chest against my back, we set off.

Chapter Ten

"What's a Gabby?" Aindreas' muffled voice startled me awake.

"Huh?" I looked around and saw vast fields around us. Aindreas, Richard, and I, along with the horses, were the only living creatures as far as I could see.

"You keep calling out the word 'Gabby' in your sleep."

I rubbed the tight muscles in my neck and yawned, a harder feat on a moving horse than I predicted. Aindreas' steady hand caught my shoulder and pulled me upright.

"Thanks." I shifted to sit better, acutely aware of how close we still were. My legs were aching, and I had no idea how long it had been since we left Magnus' house.

"A person. A 'Gabby' is a person. My closest friend actually."

"Aye, that makes sense. She kens you're here?"

"No," I hung my head, thinking of how terrified

she must have been to wake up and find out I had disappeared in my sleep.

I was so caught up in my shock of waking up in a different time that I hadn't thought of how it might have affected her. I didn't have anyone else that would've been worried, but my heart broke for Gabby. I had gotten so annoyed at how excited she was about the trip and now it was ruined for her. I would give anything to go back and hug her tightly while apologizing profusely.

"I dinnae mean to make you cry," Aindreas' voice was gruff and brisk.

"Oh no," I quickly wiped away my tears, "it wasn't you. I was thinking about how worried Gabby must be about me. And how much I miss her." I sniffled back more tears and pressed my eyes closed.

I felt an awkward pat on my back and smiled through the tears.

"It probably would be better to wait to ask you this, but I've been waiting the whole time you've been sleeping." Aindreas' voice trailed off.

I turned back to look at him and was only inches from his face. I quickly turned back around and waited for him to ask his question.

"Well, out with it, I suppose. How do you have my mam's necklace?"

"Your what?"

"The necklace you're wearing. It belonged to my

mam, and ah ken I saw it before I left my castle, tucked safely in a jewelry box."

I put my hand on the necklace and searched my mind for what to say.

"I don't know what to say," I said, honestly.

"I would most appreciate the truth. I dinnae want to kick you off my horse, but I can nae be expected to feed and protect someone stealing from me, ye ken?"

"You'll never believe me," I said.

"You would nae believe what people tell the Laird for excuses. I'm certain I'll believe you if it's the truth."

I glanced nervously over at Richard, who was riding a respectable distance from us to give the illusion of privacy, but I was certain he was close enough to hear me unless I whispered.

"Can we have a little privacy?"

"Not likely, mistress," Richard called over, confirming my suspicion.

"Anything you have to say can be said in front of Richard," Aindreas said without room for argument.

I took a deep breath and closed my eyes. The last few days played through my mind like a movie. I realized I might never see an actual movie again and felt sadder about that than I would've imagined.

"Margaret?" Aindreas said gently.

I took another deep breath and began my tale.

"First of all, that's not my name. My first name really is Mackenzie. I've never met anyone from Clan Mackenzie, so don't ask me if I'm a traitor," I eyeballed Richard and dared him to defy me. When he didn't, I continued on, "My nickname is Kenz, so maybe that would be better to call me by?"

"Margaret is a fine name," Richard said, and I felt Aindreas nod.

I sighed and told them about the experience at Castle Balfour. They both perked up at the mention of their home and became confused at what an immersive experience was.

"I should take a few steps back. I was born three hundred years from now," I cringed and looked over at Richard.

It was an incomprehensible thing to say, and Richard laughed, as one should when hearing something so ridiculous.

"Silence, Richard. Let her finish." Aindreas' voice was soft, but commanding.

"No, he was right to laugh. Why aren't you looking at me like I'm ridiculous?"

"First off, I can nae see you, just your back."

I blushed, thankful that he could only see me from behind.

"And second? I trust you. Something about you feels familiar. But you have nae answered how that necklace came to be around your neck."

"While taking a vacation at Castle Balfour, I went to a shop. It used to be run by blacksmiths, but they took up jewelry making at some point. There was a sweet old lady running the shop. Her name was Isla something."

What did Mrs. Campbell say?

"Ah yes, McMillan. Isla McMillan."

Richard stopped his horse and Aindreas backed us up a few steps. Richard's face was pale, and his hands were shaking. He reminded me of Isla McMillan, and I gasped.

"She's your descendant, isn't she?"

"Aye," Aindreas answered for his dumbfounded friend and chuckled, "I guess here is as good as any place to take a break."

He chuckled and dismounted the horse before helping me down off of it. His touch still made my stomach flutter, and I couldn't explain it away any longer.

We made our way down to a creek while Richard sat on his horse, muttering to himself.

"Is he okay?"

"He will be. It's nae every day you find out your descendants are a piece in a tapestry of woven time."

"Woven time, huh? I hadn't thought of time like a tapestry before. What made him believe me?"

Aindreas laughed again and the sound of his happiness reverberated through my heart.

"His son is the current blacksmith, and his son, Richard's grandson, will be the one to take it over. The little bairn has already started talking about how much he loves jewelry and wants to craft 'the most beautiful pieces the world has ever seen.' We've all brushed him off, but maybe there's something to that dream after all."

Aindreas grew pensive and stared at the creek.

"What is it?"

"I'll have to get the boy some money to make sure the venture is successful."

He turned and looked at me with piercing blue eyes that made my heart stop.

"He has to make it work so you find your way to me."

I touched the necklace and nodded. His eyes drifted down to the pendant, and a sad look came over his face.

"Tell me more about how that brought you here."

"Well, I'm not exactly sure how it happened. I'll tell you what I can though."

I recounted Isla's instructions and what I did before bed, making sure to include every detail I could recall.

"And then I woke up in 1722."

"In my bed." He scratched his chin and turned his

gaze back to the creek. "That's a lot to take in, learning you're someone's true love."

I nodded and bit back tears. He walked away from me without saying anything more and I was left standing there alone, feeling vulnerable and exposed. I was developing feelings for him, and it had been so foolish of me. How could he be my true love? We had only known each other for a few days, and I felt dumb for falling so fast. Of course, he didn't feel the same way.

Richard's voice traveled down the hill before either of us could say any more.

"If we want to get to a better place before it's dark, we need to keep moving."

We walked silently up the hill to meet Richard. Aindreas swung me up onto the horse with a dark look across his face, and we were off.

Chapter Eleven

The rest of the journey went a little better. Sharing my secret with Aindreas and Richard took a lot of weight off my shoulders, and I relaxed into the solidness of Aindreas behind me on the horse.

Despite our awkward encounter at the creek, we came to a silent agreement that talking was vastly superior to riding in silence. Our conversations took the form of guessing games about what the future held.

"Do men own more than one horse?"

"Most men have none."

"When do I die?"

"I don't know and that's not a fair question."

"Alright, I suppose."

They would guess a few things and then contemplate their next questions before firing at me back and forth until my head was spinning.

"I can't be telling you all of these things. What if we mess up the future?"

"You traveled here from the future. It was skewed

to begin with."

I laughed. "That's a good point. But I'm still not going to tell you everything. I don't think that's how it works."

Aindreas made a sound of protest behind me, and I couldn't help but wonder if he was acutely aware of his breath hitting the back of my neck like I was. I tried to push the thoughts aside and focus on their next barrage of questions.

"How does the castle look in your time?"

"Beautiful, it took my breath away when I first laid eyes on it."

"I'll have to make sure we up the funds to keep it maintained and nae let anything fall into ruins. It's already more than a century old. I can nae imagine it three hundred years older."

"Make sure you're not spreading your money too thin."

Richard gave me a quizzical look, "Why would you say that, mistress?"

"One of the servants at Magnus' house mentioned the money is dwindling."

Aindreas scoffed, "What a funny bit of gossip. They dinnae ken anything about my money."

Something made me uncomfortable, but perhaps it was that I wasn't used to servants gossiping. I brushed it aside and returned the conversation to the castle.

"Will we get to see the castle soon?" My mind drifted to seeing it in all its glory, still operating as it was intended.

"Nae for a while," Aindreas said brusquely, with no other explanation.

I looked over at Richard for some insight and he sighed heavily before looking at Aindreas and then back at me.

"The vicious rumors about Aindreas and his father spread to our lands early on. Someone poisoned the ears of the tenants and there was an uprising calling for Magnus to become Laird."

"Aye," Aindreas said, darkly, "I'm in a great debt to my cousin for nae taking them up on the offer the first chance he got. He's been trying to find the murderer and restore my good name."

"So you have nowhere to go that's safe?"

"Nae, I can only travel until I'm far enough away that I'm nae recognized by a soul, ye ken?"

Of course, I finally found my soulmate and there were two big hindrances that seemed impossible to ever get past - he was a fugitive who would be on the run for an indefinite amount of time, and he didn't love me back. I was thankful he couldn't see my face as a lone tear slid down my cheek.

"Margaret, did you hear me?" Aindreas said in a low whisper, and I shook my head, the hairs on my arm standing up as I realized the woods around us were silent. No birds chirping, no little animals scurrying about. Something felt wrong.

"Show yourself!" Aindreas boomed out behind me, and I stifled a scream.

While we waited for movement or a person to appear, he grabbed my waist and slid me down the side of the horse, shielding me from the threat. He nodded his head toward Richard, who moved his horse beside me and pointed to a downed log I could hide behind.

I was sick to my stomach as I watched Aindreas waiting like a sitting duck. I felt helpless and fought the urge to go back to him. What good would I do without a sword in my hand? Or any fighting skills.

A bush moved in the distance, and I held my breath. Aindreas and Richard moved their horses to be at more of a defensive stance once they identified the exact direction of the threat. A man on an impatient horse came bursting onto the scene. He had his sword drawn and looked like he was out for blood.

"What's your business?" Aindreas asked, his voice strong and unfaltering.

"Ah ken who you are," the man said with slurred speech that made my nerves skyrocket.

"You do? And who am I?"

"You're a murderer. A father killer at that. And today you die."

I put my hand over my mouth to avoid making any noise. Aindreas laughed, and Richard stole a glance back at me while none of the attention was on him. I tried to give him a reassuring smile, but could only look at him in shock. I had come too far to find Aindreas and didn't even have him yet. He couldn't die here.

The man rushed Aindreas and had his sword aimed and ready to strike him in the time Aindreas asked, "Who sent you?"

I let out a small cry, unable to hold back my fear any longer. It startled the man, and he hesitated for a second, giving Richard enough time to draw his sword and drive it through him from behind. The man collapsed forward on his horse and the horse whinnied and snorted.

Aindreas jumped down and secured the horse so it wouldn't ride off with the man's body. Richard had his back to me as he dismounted his own horse and stared in the opposite direction of the man.

Seeing me behind the log, Aindreas rushed over. "Sorry about that. I dinnae have time to warn you before I yelled. Are you okay?"

He cupped my face in his hands and looked me up and down.

"I'm fine, really. Are you okay? How's Richard?"

Aindreas reached out for my hand, and we walked over to Richard together.

"You dinnae have to kill him," Aindreas looked at Richard with worry in his eyes, "but I thank you. You saved my life. I'll take care of the body."

Richard's hands were still shaking, and I was certain that was the first time he had killed anyone. I had a sneaking suspicion he did it to save Aindreas' conscience. I stepped forward and put my hands on Richard's shoulders. He looked up at me with a depth of sadness in his eyes that made my heart break for him. His loyalty ran deep and true. He fell into my arms, and I hugged him tightly as he let his emotions out in one quick sob. He took off his glasses, rubbed his eyes, and cleared his throat, wasting no more time than necessary.

"What do we do now, my Laird?"

"Ah dinnae ken. I wish I could send word to Magnus and find out which direction would be better."

"Did he tell you to go this way?"

"Aye, he says there are allies nae too far from here.

Aindreas' trust in Magnus made my stomach uneasy. I knew he wouldn't listen to me about it, though. His belief that his cousin was on his side was deeply rooted and some girl from the future he'd just met wasn't going to change his mind.

Chapter Twelve

When my body felt like it couldn't take another moment of travel, we made it to a village that didn't recognize Aindreas. Richard went ahead of us and found a place to stay, but Aindreas was convinced we should keep going toward the allies Magnus had told him about. In an effort to buy time, I talked him into at least staying one night.

Walking beside the horses, we wound through the people bustling about with their everyday life. The smell of fire and meats roasting filled the air and my stomach growled.

"I suppose it would be nice to rest for a night."

I turned and looked at Aindreas. His face was haggard and worn looking. His eyes, despite their crystal blue color, were heavy and disheartened. I reached out and put my hand on his arm. He gave me a weary smile and my heart ached for him.

"While we're here, we need to get to the bottom of how information is spreading about where you'll be and find your father's killer," Richard said, his voice still finding its strength after the day's events.

"Aye," Aindreas said with a sigh.

"The inn we're staying at is run by a man who seems to know everyone's business. We could talk to him and see what he has heard."

"No! That will just draw attention to us being here," I cried.

"We have no better option," Aindreas hung his head.

I started to object, but I could see he believed that whole-heartedly. Before I could have said anything, Richard spoke up.

"Aye, it is our best option. We'll be gone before they can tell anyone we were here."

It didn't feel like a good solution to me, but I could see there was no use in protesting it. At least I was in my comfort zone – being ignored by men who thought they knew better than me but were unable to see the forest through the trees.

Richard hurriedly told us that he had told a trivial lie to secure our rooms and not draw attention.

"When I mentioned we needed rooms for two men and a lady, it raised some eyebrows. They asked me if the lady was a," Richard lowered his voice to an almost inaudible level, "a lady of pleasure. I assured them most heartily that she is nae such thing."

He puffed up his chest indignantly and I hid my smile.

"So they said, 'well whose wife is she?' I was unprepared. I dinnae kent they would be asking me such questions and that those would be my only options to answer with. I told them you was Aindreas' wife, and they accepted that without further question and gave us two rooms for the three of us."

He looked at both of us apologetically.

"Aye, tis fine. I'll be a perfect gentleman," Aindreas winked at me, and I felt my cheeks flush.

"Let's get some food before I hear her stomach grumbling anymore," Richard jerked his thumb towards me, and I started to say something about how rude that was before my stomach grumbled again. I followed them into the tavern with no complaint.

Every eye was on me as we entered, and I tried to look away from the stares. I'm sure I stood out like a racoon trying to blend in with kittens. Even as I averted my eyes, their looks bore into my skin and were hard to ignore.

Aindreas ordered for the two of us, which would have been romantic if he knew anything about me.

"Am I not allowed to see my options?" I said, while the server was still standing there.

Aindreas looked at me in disbelief, "Nae, you'll like it."

I folded my arms across my chest and matched his look. "I doubt it."

The server's mouth was hanging open and Rich-

ENTWINED IN TIME

ard's eyes were wide. They were no doubt appalled at his brazen attempt to control what I was eating.

"What are your other options?" I politely asked the server.

She looked over at Aindreas and hesitated.

"She'll be having what I ordered," he grumbled, and the server practically tripped over her own feet to head to the back.

"What just happened?" I asked, furiously.

"You just went against your *husband's* word. Dinnae do that again," Aindreas' voice was gruff and his words final.

I was seething, but sat back and waited for my food to arrive.

Dinner conversation was kept light because the prying eyes were accompanied by nosy ears. I also wasn't exactly in the mood to discuss anything with them.

After we ate, Aindreas asked if I wanted to take a stroll around the village to get some supplies for the rest of our journey. I obliged, figuring some fresh air would be nice. Plus, it wasn't every day I got to experience life in 18th century Scotland, unless this was to be my life from now on.

I wanted to clear up the air around him ordering food for me and explain that it wasn't appreciated at all, but I hesitated around the subject. I didn't know him well enough to know how to approach it.

73

Then out of nowhere, Aindreas stopped walking and looked at me, "You can't do that."

"What?"

"You can't go against something I've said, it's nae how we do things here."

I quietly nodded, and we kept walking.

"When we get back to my homelands, we can figure this all out. I hate to tell someone who has traveled through centuries to find me that I can nae be with her. Especially when she's as pretty as you."

I felt a little bit of my anger float away as he turned his sincere eyes in my direction. I bit my lip and nodded as my eyes filled up with tears. He gave me a sad half smile that made my heart ache even more than I thought possible.

First, time was separating us without either of us knowing. Now I had him right in front of me and couldn't do anything about it until his past demons were put to rest.

We walked around the village, working on not drawing any unnecessary attention to ourselves as Aindreas gathered what he needed. We filled our time with easy conversation, but our unspoken words hung over the air above us like a cloud threatening to burst.

By the end of the evening, the feelings I had been trying to ignore were winning out. His smile made my knees weak, and he had taken so much delight in showing me things I had never seen before. It baffled him every time I said I hadn't heard of something, and he was more than happy to introduce me to new things.

"I can see you're getting tired, Margaret." His eyes glistened in the firelight from fires that burned every few feet now that the sun was going down. He was reveling in our shared secret about my name, but I longed for him to be able to call me by my real name.

Every time he said Margaret, I felt like more of a fraud. The wrong name. The wrong time. The wrong place. Nothing felt right except being with him.

Would that be enough to sustain me for the rest of my life?

Richard guided us to our room and apologized again. I smiled at him and assured him I was okay. Aindreas echoed my words and opened the door for me.

I entered the room and saw one bed about the size of a double bed in the middle of the room. A fireplace was blazing, and the toasty room was a welcome relief from the crisp air outside.

Aindreas began removing some of the bedding and setting it up on the floor.

"We are *married*, you know. Sleep up here," I

said playfully, hoping my words were lighthearted enough and didn't sound desperate.

He shook his head and carried on with his task.

"I'm fine on the floor," Aindreas roughly fluffed up his uncomfortable looking bedding and flopped his head down.

"What would it hurt if you slept up here?" I tried to not sound whiny and pathetic, but it hurt being rejected like that.

"It would nae be right for me to sleep in your bed, nae matter how badly I want to."

"Oh," I said softly, and rolled over, knowing sleep would be hard to find after that revelation.

Chapter Thirteen

I woke up to the sound of Aindreas and Richard debating something. Tuning in to the exact words, I could hear it was about which person was responsible for which thing.

It was so clear that Magnus was behind all of it. He knew where Aindreas would be at all times because he was the one telling him where to go. He was spreading rumors that his loose-lipped servants told me, and he gave me the creeps. The last point wasn't exactly evidence, but it had to count for something.

Aindreas continued to hold steadfast to his belief that his cousin was an upstanding man because he didn't try to take the lands from him when he clearly could have. I thought he was an underhanded con-man who was playing a long game, but would want it to end soon, especially based on the man who had been sent to kill Aindreas. Who else would have been behind it?

We were only safe at the inn because Magnus didn't know we were there. It wasn't in his plan he told Aindreas before we left, so it was a curveball he didn't account for. I worried about what would be waiting for us when we got to the supposed allies Aindreas was itching to reach.

The days of travel and being in a new place were taking a toll on me, and the fear of the unknown ahead of us was bothering me. I was done listening to their unproductive discussions when too many things were at stake.

"Why can't you guys see who is behind this?"

Aindreas and Richard kept their heads pressed close together, not hearing a word I said.

I felt my blood boiling. I was sick and tired of not being listened to and their lack of observation skills was going to get us killed. Picking up a rock, I tossed it to the center of the table where it landed with a deep thud, scarring the surface.

"Listen to me!" I said through gritted teeth.

"What's wrong?" Aindreas looked up, startled by my outburst, "You sound a wee bit frustrated."

"Yes, of course I'm frustrated. I'm in a time that's not my own. I'm being called a name that's not my own. And no one is taking me seriously because I'm a woman."

Aindreas stared at me, and his mouth dropped open, "I dinnae have any idea."

"No, of course you didn't. Why would it matter to you?"

I gathered my skirts about me and stormed out of

the room. It felt dramatic, but I was tired. I had no amenities I was used to, and even in a time and place where no one knew me, I was being dismissed.

Cursing under my breath, I made my way out of the inn and over to a small creek and sat at the edge of it. I ran my fingers through the cool water, still fuming.

A hand clasped my shoulder, and I jumped.

"Tis me," a warm, familiar voice said.

"Oh, Aindreas." I exhaled a sigh of relief that it hadn't been someone from an enemy clan. By running down to the creek, I had acted every bit the foolish woman they thought I was.

He pulled me in for a hug and I welcomed the comfort of an embrace, even if he was the one person I wanted to get away from in the moment.

"I'm sorry, I-"

"Nae, tis I who am sorry. You're right. I should have listened. One of the things I hated most about my father was how he treated my mam. He never gave her attention and would brush her aside without thought."

He looked down at me, his eyebrows furrowed together. "I did the same thing to you. Can you forgive me, Kenz?"

His use of my nickname, the only form of my name he could use without drawing unnecessary bad attention to us, was not lost on me. He was looking at me patiently, waiting for my response.

"Yes, of course I can forgive you. I'm sorry too. You know the customs and what's expected, and I know nothing. It wouldn't hurt if I let you take the lead every once in a while."

"Aye," he brushed a lock of hair out of my face, "but not too often. It would do me some good to follow your advice most of the time."

"Smart man," I said, and he chuckled.

He pulled me tighter against him and my stomach fluttered as the distance between our faces shrunk to nothing. The blue sky behind Aindreas brought out the color of his eyes and he stroked my cheek with his thumb before leaning in to press his lips against mine. I closed my eyes and melted into his embrace.

In that moment, I became Scottish and a citizen of the 18th century. There was no going back for me now.

We would defeat whoever was turning the clans against Aindreas and we would be victorious.

We headed back to our rooms and I felt lighter than I had in days.

I smiled at Richard across the table from me. For as much as Aindreas was tall and stoic, Richard was small and mousy. He was loyal though, and the only one who was standing by Aindreas in all of Scotland.

"Tell me again why you think it's Magnus?" He peered over his glasses and folded his hands in front of him.

"A few things stood out to me. First, Magnus' servants gossiped to me about Aindreas- they had to get that information from somewhere. Then, the man who tried to attack us knew right where to find us. Who told Aindreas which route to take? Magnus. On top of that, he also gives me an awful feeling."

This last statement made me sound like a woman ruled by her emotions, something that wouldn't hold up against anyone. Aindreas grabbed my hand and nodded at me, his gentle eyes coaxing me on.

"When I met him, he didn't seem like he was on our side. His words were unsettling, and I don't trust a thing he says."

"Aye, I agree with that." Richard nodded pensively.

"He has the most to gain if Aindreas is taken down and I think his initial refusal to turn against Aindreas was just a ploy for people to trust him."

"How should we take him down?" Richard's full attention was on me now and I shifted in my seat.

"I don't know that part."

Aindreas bristled his eyebrows together and bit the corner of his mouth. "I dinnae want any bloodshed if it can be avoided. He's still my cousin. Even if that means nae to him, it still means something to me."

My heart swelled at the gentle man next to me. I knew he would do what it took to defend his castle and lands, but knowing that he would prefer it happen peacefully impressed me. He wasn't anything like what I had pictured fierce, battle worn Larids to be like.

"She's right, ye ken," Richard said, taking his glasses off and folding them on the table.

"Aye, tis Magnus. It's the only thing that makes sense."

Richard nodded and stared forlornly toward Mackenzie's sleeping form.

"How will you keep her safe?"

"I have to send her back." Aindreas' mouth was set in a hard, straight line.

Richard wrung his hands and fretted about the room. "She won't like that you managed her like this. I dinnae ken what women are like in her time, but they're not like our women are here."

"What choice do I have?" Aindreas hung his head, "I'd never forgive myself." He choked on the last two words and Richard stepped forward to put his hand on his friend and Laird's shoulder.

A rustling caught their attention, and they

looked up to see Mackenzie moving in her sleep, her lips pursed like she was frantically trying to work out something in her dreams.

"She's stirring. If you're going to make a move, you must do it now. Hopefully what your heart wants will be the right thing to send her home." He looked nervous and glanced at the sleeping figure across the room before turning his back to give them privacy.

Aindreas knelt down beside Mackenzie's bed and fought the urge to take her hand in his for the moment. He tucked a stray strand of hair behind her ear and closed his eyes as he pressed his lips against her forehead. He touched the pendant resting on her chest and imagined what his heart wanted most of all–Mackenzie back in her own time. Safe.

He gripped her hand for a moment, no longer scared of waking her up. The necklace shimmered slightly, and he forced himself to let go of her hand.

And then she was gone.

Aindreas let out a small sob that he quickly swallowed and turned into a resolve. A fire burned inside him, and he would not rest until his cousin was stopped.

Chapter Fourteen

"Mackenzie!"

Gabby's hand was holding mine, and I jumped out of bed, frantically spinning around in circles and disappointed to be back in a clearly modernized version of the castle.

"He sent me back," I said in a daze.

I looked out the window and saw cars outside. I ran to the bathroom and saw plumbing. There was a light switch on the wall. I flipped it up and down before running out of my room.

Gabby was hot on my heels.

"Kenz!"

I couldn't turn back around. I needed to get to him, to see his face, and know he was safe.

"Who sent you back?" Gabby's voice sounded as panicked as I felt. I couldn't stop my feet from moving and quickly found myself in front of his portrait. Running my hand along his cheek, my body let out an involuntary sob and fell to the ground.

Gabby dropped to the ground next to me and

began rubbing my back. A gentle shushing sound was quieting my mind, but I still couldn't concentrate.

Why would Aindreas send me back? I was prepared to fight right alongside him. He didn't trust me. He probably still suspected I was a Mackenzie and had just been nice to me to lull me into a false sense of security.

"Kenz, talk to me. You're scaring me and it won't be long before someone comes in and checks on us."

I nodded and let her lead me to her room. The castle was a mix of new and old, and I had to close my eyes as she guided me down the halls, not wanting a reminder of the past.

My head was still spinning when we reached her room, and I put my hand on the necklace resting on my chest to steady myself. At least the necklace was real. I felt down for the satchel at my waist and saw that I still had the coins and a flower he had given me while walking around the market. It was still fresh.

I absentmindedly tossed the coins between my hands and stared at their glittering surfaces.

"Why do those look new?"

I looked up and saw Gabby staring at the coins with wide eyes. I tossed her one and she held it like it was going to explode.

"Kenz, talk, now." She pushed me down into a sitting chair and promptly sat down across from me.

"He sent me back." It seemed like that was all my mind could focus on.

"Yes, you said that. Who sent you back?" Gabby's voice was measured and patient, but I could see the impatience and fear on her face.

"Aindreas," I whispered, afraid to say his name louder.

"Who's Aindreas?" Gabby's eyes were about to pop out of their sockets, and I knew she knew exactly who I was talking about. She slowly shook her head and stared at me.

I nodded and let the tears flow freely from my eyes. I didn't have time to hold back how I felt about him any longer. I needed to put all my efforts towards helping him figure out how Magnus was getting away with betraying him and how to defeat him so we could live in peace.

Maybe peace was a fantasy, but regardless of that, I needed to get back to him. I had been back in my time for less than a half hour and it was far worse living in a world where he was already dead.

"I need to get back to him."

"I don't understand," Gabby was still shaking her head.

"I don't either. It's this necklace, though. It belonged to his mom who passed away. She must have put her dying wish in it and it helped me find my true love and it was Aindreas. It sent me back to his time. And there's this guy Magnus, it's his cousin. He tries to control Aindreas, but Aindreas was finally seeing it and about to stand up to him. He's so strong and such a natural leader. You'd really like him. You'll probably never meet him. I might never see him again."

"Kenz, you're rambling. Start over."

I filled her in on how my last few days had been. It didn't really seem like that much time had passed, but it felt like I was telling her about an entire lifetime. I kept stopping to add in details as I remembered them, and she gently rushed me along to finish the story.

"Why did he send you back?"

"I don't know. I think he sent me back because I was overstepping. Wait, you actually believe my story?"

Gabby shrugged. "I've been in Scotland looking for my missing best friend. I've heard theory after theory as superstitious people have come forward saying they saw you floating through the air, held up by fairies. I'm so happy you're safe. I believe you. Plus, you smell and look different."

I lifted my arm to smell my armpit, and she laughed. "I didn't say you smell bad, just different. Kind of florally and fresh. So, he sent you back because you were overstepping, and you still want to help?"

"Yeah, wait, no." I flashed back to the kiss we had shared and the look in his eyes when he listened to my theories about Magnus. Had that really only been the last couple of nights? Well, technically three hundred years ago. The back and forth were messing with my head.

I choked back a sob as I realized what was going on. "He sent me back to keep me safe. He's going to go after Magnus with only Richard by his side."

"It'll be okay, we'll figure out what we can from here."

"No, Gabby, you don't understand. It's truly just two men against what seems like all of Scotland. It's just Aindreas, and a guy named Richard against several clans."

"I may not understand that part, but I do know you'll figure out exactly what to do. You were born for this. There's an entire library at our disposal that might hold answers."

"Okay, how are we going to get away with snooping around?"

"Well, Mrs. Campbell is out for the day and almost all the guests have gone home. They usually have a few days to reset the castle and start over before the next group comes, but I said I refused to leave. I *may* have threatened a lawsuit since my best friend was seemingly kidnapped in her sleep."

"Effective," I mused, and she nodded.

"One of the guys who was a guest when we got here, Mr. Patterson, was convinced you were Lady Balfour. He wouldn't shut up about it after you went missing and at the time, I was so relieved when he left. He said he lives a short plane ride away and would be willing to talk to me as soon as I came to my senses." She rifled through her purse and pulled out something I couldn't see from my seat, "He left a business card, we could call him and see what he knows."

I felt dizzy and had to sit down.

Lady Balfour?

Me?

Chapter Fifteen

"You're the one who unites them."

I looked at her incredulously. "Me? The one who gets passed over for promotions? No one takes me seriously. How do you expect me to believe I unite feuding clans?"

Gabby shrugged, "You give them a pretty rousing speech."

I tried to grab the book she was getting her information from away from her, but she pulled it away.

"Nope, if you just memorize the words, it won't come from the heart like it needs to. You're about to be Lady Balfour. You've got this. Or are you already Lady Balfour since you guys would've gotten married like three centuries ago? How does this work?"

I rubbed my temples and groaned, "I don't know. I'm trying not to give that part too much thought so my brain doesn't explode trying to work it all out. The me you're talking to couldn't even be considered his girlfriend."

Gabby made a sympathetic noise and left the room to get us some more food. The hours drifted by as we searched the books for proof Magnus was the betrayer. Anything I could prove when I went back would help build a case against him and get the clans on our side.

Castle Balfour's library had an extensive collection of accounts by studious historians who recorded the most minute details. I needed a book that gave an account from the other clans about how Magnus lied to them.

I was barely two bites into my sandwich when Gabby squealed, and I choked on the dry bread.

"You wrote this!"

"Hm?" I said, trying to dislodge the food from my throat with some water.

"This book. It's written by you." She held up a small, inconspicuous looking book, its spine cracked and the words on the front faded with time. She pointed to the bottom corner of the book, and I saw KENZ stamped into the bottom right corner.

She handed me the book and I tilted the cover in every direction to try and make out the rest of the words printed on it.

Sounding it out as they became visible at different angles, I read, "A Manifesto Against Magnus" and felt my pulse quicken.

I squealed and gingerly opened the book. Its spine snapped and groaned from sitting in a castle library for centuries.

Page after page was filled with accounts from tenants and members of other clans about how Magnus had extorted them. I skimmed through it and gasped when I read the final words on the last page.

"Gabby, you found it," I whispered and looked up at her, unable to say anything more.

She nodded and started crying, "I wish it would have taken us more than a day so I could have had more time with you."

I nodded, and we held each other tightly.

"I know you have to go back to him. From what I read in there, these people need you."

"I don't even know them yet. If it weren't for Aindreas, I would stay here in a heartbeat."

"I know, I've seen your future with him." Her eyes were filled with tears that she smiled through.

I was lucky to have a friend like her and the thought of leaving felt a part of me was dying.

I tried to still my nerves and get ready for bed like it was any regular night. I took a little extra time showering in an actual shower, even if it was still frigid, and dressed myself in my freshly laundered clothes. Gabby was still in awe of how much more there was to my outfit than the modern-day replicas and watched the entire process intently, helping where needed.

"How will I find my way back to him?" I whispered, tears in my eyes.

Gabby patted my shoulder, and turned me around to face her. "Here, I know I told you not to look at anything more that would give away the future, but I think this would help you."

She pulled a piece of paper out of a folder next to her and I gasped when I saw a reprint of a wedding portrait of Aindreas and myself. My hair was swept up, the necklace was around my neck, and the two of us were looking into each other's eyes. The painter captured the exact curve of Aindreas' hands and the blueness of his eyes.

I couldn't explain how I'd fallen in love with him in such a short, tumultuous time. It felt like we had lived several lives in the course of a few days and this portrait showed me there was so much more left to our story.

I gave Gabby the tightest hug, and we both cried into each other's arms, knowing we may never see each other again.

"What will you tell everyone?"

"That my best friend found a Scottish Laird and ran away to live in his castle for the rest of time."

Her smile was bittersweet and tugged at my heart, but the tug to the past was pulling me harder.

"Thank you, for everything." I kissed her cheek and handed her the portrait back.

She closed her eyes and big tears fell down her cheeks.

"Goodbye, my friend, Lady Balfour." There was no mocking in her voice as she curtsied and backed out of the door.

I got into bed and held the pendant in my hand, pressing it to my chest and repeating the same steps I'd taken before.

"Take me to him," I whispered, and closed my eyes.

Chapter Sixteen

"Why did you send me back? Why don't you trust me?" I hit my fist against his solid chest, and he softly held my hand up to his mouth. He kissed my palm and looked at me for a moment, the silence killing me.

"Can I nae enjoy you being back for a moment?" He threw his arms open and raised his eyebrows.

I sighed and fell into his open arms, feeling a comfort and strength I had never known.

"Kenz," he said slowly, "I do trust you. That's nae why I sent you back."

"Then why?" Tears of frustration soaked my face as I thought about how scared I had been to never see him again, and he futilely wiped them away

"I could nae lose you. I've lost so much and the thought of losing you felt like my body was being ripped in two."

"I can take care of myself," I said with determination, but his words made me swoon. I had been all wrong about how he felt.

"Maybe in your time, but nae here. Here, I need to take care of you."

I raised my eyebrow and pulled the book out of my satchel.

"What's this?"

"Your battle strategy."

"I told you, I do nae want to kill anyone."

I looked up at him and thrust the book into his hand, opening it to the first page. He studied it for a moment, his eyes growing larger with each page he flipped to.

"See? There's a benefit to knowing someone from the future."

"These are confessions from many of the men who are allied with Magnus. He's forcing them?"

"Yep, it looks like he's extorting them. So many of things aren't even that big of offenses. He doesn't have an army against you. He has people desperate to keep themselves safe. They just want to be farmers and live in peace. These are your people, not his. Flip to the final page."

He obliged and I watched his mouth silently repeating the words he was reading. His eyes grew wider with every word he read.

"Magnus killed my father? This is more than enough to convict him," Aindreas' eyes glistened, and I stepped forward to hug him again, thankful to be back in his arms, even if we had a lot of work ahead of us before we would be posing for a wedding portrait.

"Yes, there's just one problem. They haven't made those confessions yet."

"Well, let's go get them." Aindreas kissed my forehead and put his hand on his hilt, nodding to Richard.

The two men ran out of the room and slammed the door behind them. I stood there, not knowing what to do with myself, and suddenly the door burst open.

"Coming?" Aindreas had his eyebrows raised.

With wide eyes and a quick nod, I ran through the door and walked next to him while he discussed plans with Richard.

"When these men confess, there will be nae need to kill Magnus. The clans will see to it that he pays," Richard said excitedly.

Aindreas nodded and I could see it relieved him to not have to take care of his cousin himself, but the mixed feelings of knowing he would be the one to expose him weighed heavily on his mind.

I grabbed his hand, and he turned to meet my eyes. "I know this isn't exactly how things are done, but I know that if I address everyone, it will work."

"But it's my job," he said resolutely.

"Then let's do it together."

"I can nae argue with someone who knows the future," he said with a laugh, and we came up with a plan to get the word out quickly.

Chapter Seventeen

I took a deep inhale and almost passed out. My nerves were fried, and my knees were shaking. I had been fretting over what I would say ever since the first of the clans started arriving. Aindreas put his hand on the small of my back to steady me and we looked at each other before looking out at the mass of people in front of us who had traveled as quickly as they could. I took that as confirmation they were just as desperate for change as we were.

"Hello, everyone. We've asked you to come here today to discuss Magnus Balfour," I said in my loudest voice. A murmur of whispers wove through the crowd, no doubt remarking on my strange dialect and my choice to cut straight to the chase. If the book hidden in my satchel was any indication, these people were terrified of Magnus.

I looked out at the sea of faces in front of me and saw hard-working, gentle people who didn't deserve what Magnus was doing to them. A fiery passion built up in my body. Clearing my throat, I looked as many people in the eyes as I could, hoping they would feel the sincerity of my words, even if I sounded more than a little funny to them.

"Aindreas Balfour has been wrongly accused of killing his father. I have word that some of you here today know who the real murderer is. And I know that he has forced you to align with him for fear of losing what you have. I am here to assure you that we can live differently. We don't have to live in fear of threats and coercion. We can return to farming and dealing with other dangers together, as a united front. We may have differences, but I hope one thing we can agree on is this man next to me. I have only known Aindreas a brief time and I can see how wonderful he is. If you've ever met him, I'm certain you know too. He is a treasure and shouldn't be taken down like this."

My voice faltered and Aindreas gave my hand a squeeze, his smile reassuring me and giving me strength to keep going.

"An alliance with Clan Balfour, with Aindreas at the helm, is an alliance that will last for ages, if not all time. With the strength of our numbers, we can take down the real enemy and restore peace between the clans."

The crowd was silent. Their eyes were shifting back and forth, and I hoped my words would propel at least one person to step forward and break the ice.

I gripped Aindreas hand, and he squeezed mine in response.

"It'll all be okay, mo cridhe," his blue eyes sparkled with hope and the first man stepped forward.

All eyes were on him as he made his way to the front of the crowd and stopped in front of Aindreas. Placing his hand over his heart and dropping to his knees, I couldn't make out all of his words, but the sincerity behind them rang out across the crowd and one-by-one, others walked up and followed suite.

We stood there for hours as each person pledged their life and allegiance to Clan Balfour. I knew it wasn't customary for me to be crying, but I couldn't help the tears falling from my eyes when I looked over and saw the relief and joy on Aindreas' face.

Now that the threat against Aindreas was so small, we could finally return home to Castle Balfour.

Thank you for reading
Entwined in Time!

Head to www.TaylorClaremont.com for the latest news on books two and three!

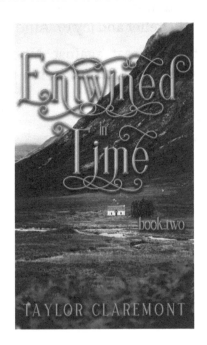

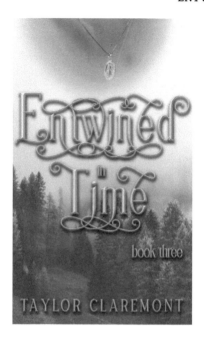